C'est la Vie

Alison M. Jablonski

Archway Publishing books may be ordered through booksellers or by contacting:

Archway Publishing
1663 Liberty Drive
Bloomington, IN 47403
www.archwaypublishing.com
844-669-3957

ISBN: 978-1-6657-2686-3 (sc)
ISBN: 978-1-6657-2687-0 (hc)
ISBN: 978-1-6657-2688-7 (e)

Print information available on the last page.

Archway Publishing rev. date: 08/12/2022

C'est
la Vie

Where, oh where, is my little fat cat? She was right by my side— but then flew like a bat! Shot out of my sight, stung by a bee, which was nipped by our dog as the dog tried to pee!

Now all are aware cats know ev'ry
way to deceive and beguile,
to make mischief all day;
to coax and connive with favorable sway
their loving masters come what may.

Well, finally found was my "sweet little cat." She was out in the garden, chasing a rat! I threw up my hands, screaming, "Mon Dieu! Quel alors!" for the rat was headed for my open back door!

I jumped high in the air to avoid the black creature which went down with a thud, right under my sneaker! The cat was quite pleased as she snatched that dam rat, leaving me to find both the rat and "le chat!"

I looked all around, checked all her cat places,
not wanting to find neither cat nor rat faces.
In fatigue, I dropped into my favorite chair,
to calm my spent nerves and to
smooth down my hair.

All of a sudden, a movement so small, from an item I had bought at the mall. A treasure it was, a straw hat, you see, With a cute flip-up brim— it was sweet as could be.
A blue gross grain ribbon encircled the crown, "le chapeau, tres jolie," was the talk of the town! But it lay on the floor not where it'd been set, far from the harm of playful house pets.

But I still had to find the cat and the rat. And I did; they were both found right under my hat! I cried, "Oh merde!" (Excuse my French, "sil vous plait!!") There was naught I could do but observe the malais. Both cat and rat were tumbling around, becoming entangled; making strange sounds.

But my hat, oh my hat!
It lay all in a ruin;
bits of ribbon and straw, all around, lay strewn.
Both the cat and the rat stopped their mad tryst,
looked at me and emitted a big, loud, long hisst.

I grabbed a broom and swung in a fit,
not really caring what I might hit.
Cat, hat, rat—no difference to me.

My attitude was, what will be, "C'est la vie!" After all, life is full of curves and surprises, Despite all our plans, including surmises! We're easily played by Fate and her minions, who taunt us with maybe's and change our decisions.

Thus, I say with a bit of chagrin,
Take life with some sugar—
and put on a grin!

Oh, . . . and always remember:
Whatever we have, whether given or bought,
put altogether, it's all for naught.
And we should admit, though
in the end we may sigh,
one fine day, it'll all go bye-bye!

Printed in the United States
by Baker & Taylor Publisher Services